This book
belongs to

_____

For my family—
home is always where you are
—K. H.

BEACH LANE BOOKS
An imprint of Simon & Schuster Children's Publishing Division
1230 Avenue of the Americas, New York, New York 10020
Text © 2022 by Cynthia Rylant
Illustration © 2022 by Katie Harnett
Book design by Lauren Rille and Lissi Erwin © 2022 by Simon & Schuster, Inc.
All rights reserved, including the right of reproduction in whole or in part in any form.
BEACH LANE BOOKS and colophon are trademarks of Simon & Schuster, Inc.
For information about special discounts for bulk purchases,
please contact Simon & Schuster Special Sales
at 1-866-506-1949 or business@simonandschuster.com.
The Simon & Schuster Speakers Bureau can bring authors to your live event.
For more information or to book an event, contact the Simon & Schuster Speakers Bureau
at 1-866-248-3049 or visit our website at www.simonspeakers.com.
The text for this book was set in Goldana Script and Excelsior.
The illustrations for this book were rendered in gouache paint and colored pencils.
Manufactured in China
0122 SCP
First Edition
10 9 8 7 6 5 4 3 2 1
Library of Congress Cataloging-in-Publication Data
Names: Rylant, Cynthia, author. | Harnett, Katie, illustrator.
Title: Home is where the birds sing / Cynthia Rylant ; illustrated by Katie Harnett.
Description: First edition. | New York : Beach Lane Books, [2022] | Audience: Ages 0–8. |
Audience: Grades 2–3. | Summary: Illustrations and text celebrate the many things—both big and
small—that make a place feel like home.
Identifiers: LCCN 2021022429 (print) | LCCN 2021022430 (ebook) | ISBN 9781534449572 (hardcover) |
ISBN 9781534449589 (ebook)
Subjects: CYAC: Home—Fiction. | Belonging (Social psychology)—Fiction. | LCGFT: Picture books.
Classification: LCC PZ7.R982 Hs 2022 (print) | LCC PZ7.R982 (ebook) | DDC [E]—dc23
LC record available at https://lccn.loc.gov/2021022429
LC ebook record available at https://lccn.loc.gov/2021022430

Home Is Where the Birds Sing

written by
Cynthia Rylant

illustrated by
Katie Harnett

Beach Lane Books

New York   London   Toronto   Sydney   New Delhi

Home is where
you come in from the rain.

And where you have a little nap,
after a bite.

It is where you are welcome!

Home is where someone calls you "sweetie" or "dear" or a dozen other names for love.

It is where you wake up and look at pictures on the wall.

And where you have blankets.

Home is where you freshen up!
(Or hide if you don't want to freshen up.)

It is where your friends can find you.

Home is where there are stories to tell

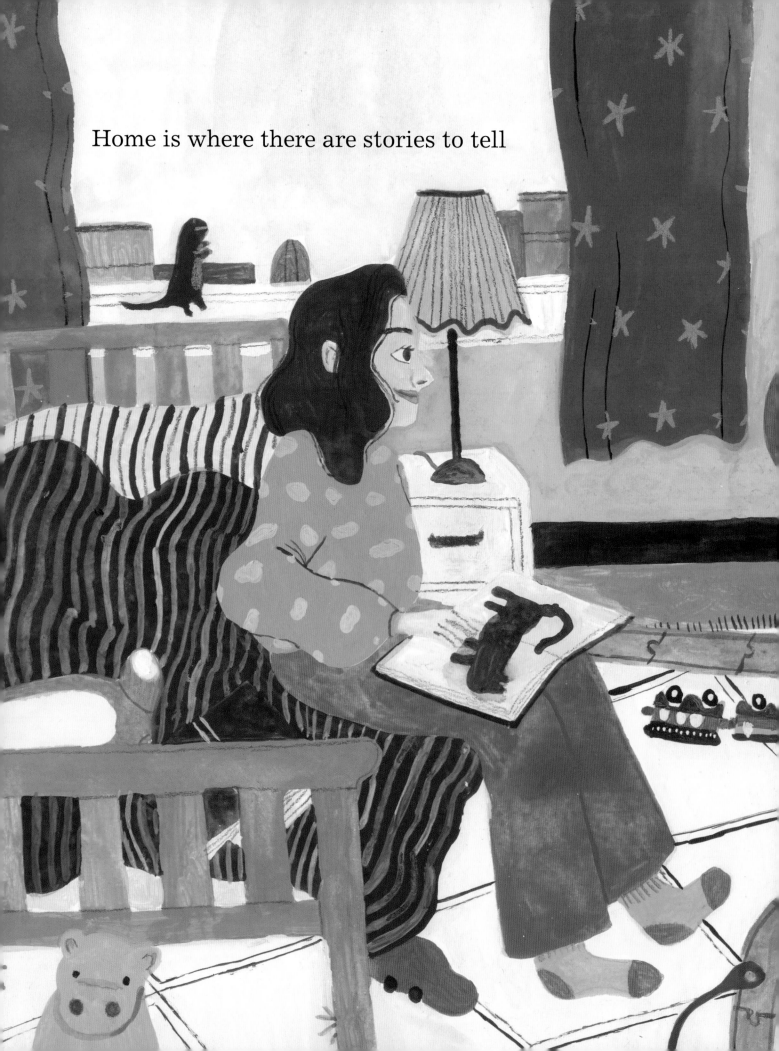

and stories to hear.

It is where your own story starts.

Home is where
the birds sing.

And where the moon shines on you at night.

It is where you will run,
if you ever need to run.

And where you will find
the door wide open.

Home is where
everything waits for you,

waits for you,

waits for you.

And when you come back
from anywhere,

it is where you will feel at home.

Because you are.